WHY WAR HAPPENED

WHAT CAUSED WORLD WAR I?

BY ROBYN HARDYMAN

Gareth Stevens
PUBLISHING

Please visit our website, www.garethstevens.com.
For a free color catalog of all our high-quality books,
call toll free 1-800-542-2595 or fax 1-877-542-2596.

Cataloging-in-Publication Data
Names: Hardyman, Robyn.
Title: What caused World War I? / Robyn Hardyman.
Description: New York : Gareth Stevens Publishing, 2017. | Series: Why war happened | Includes index.
Identifiers: ISBN 9781482451887 (pbk.) | ISBN 9781482451825 (library bound) | ISBN 9781482451719 (6 pack)
Subjects: LCSH: World War, 1914-1918--Juvenile literature. | World War, 1914-1918--Causes--Juvenile literature.
Classification: LCC D522.7 H37 2017 | DDC 940.3--dc23

First Edition

Published in 2017 by
Gareth Stevens Publishing
111 East 14th Street, Suite 349
New York, NY 10003

Produced by Calcium
Editors: Sarah Eason and Harriet McGregor
Designer: Jessica Moon
Picture researcher: Harriet McGregor

Picture credits: Cover: Getty: Fototeca Storica Nazionale (photo), Shutterstock: kasha_malasha (bkgrd). Insides: Shutterstock: Susan Law Cain 41, Oleg Doroshin 12, Everett Historical 5, 7, 9, 11, 17, 18, 19, 23, 27, 31, 33, 35, 37, 38, 40, 42, 43, Oleg Golovnev 13, Willequet Manuel 44; Wikimedia Commons: Le Patriote Illustré/Loki11 20, Bernard Partridge 15, Karl Tröstl 25, U.S. Army 29.

Printed in the United States of America
CPSIA compliance information: Batch #CS16GS: For further information contact Gareth Stevens, New York, New York at 1-800-542-2595.

CONTENTS

Words in the glossary appear in **bold** type the first time they are used in the text.

CHAPTER 1

WORLD WAR I

There was no single event that caused World War I (1914–1918). By the time war broke out, in the summer of 1914, a series of events in Europe had made a military conflict inevitable. These events were caused by political changes that had happened over the previous 40 years. There were several powerful countries in the region, all competing for power.

The war was fought between two groups of countries. On one side were the Allied Powers of Britain, France, Russia, Serbia, and Belgium. On the other side were the **Central Powers** of Germany, Austria-Hungary, Bulgaria, and the Turkish Empire. The war was fought mainly in Europe, but it affected people across the world because soldiers from many countries joined up to fight for one side or the other.

Once the war started, many people thought it would be over quickly, but they were wrong. The war developed in ways that made it very difficult to bring it to an end, as neither side could secure a victory. At the start, the war was fought with

POPPIES FOR REMEMBRANCE

In total, 65 million troops from around the world fought in World War I. More than 8 million of them were killed. Often men fought in long trenches dug into the ground, a few hundred yards away from their opponents. The land between them was blasted and churned to mud by the fighting. After the war, poppies that had once grown in these fields began to grow again, as their seeds were brought to life by the disturbance in the ground. Poppies soon became a powerful symbol of remembrance of all the men who lost their lives.

This liquid fire flamethrower gun was a weapon first used in World War I. It fired burning fuel.

old technology that had been used in wars in the nineteenth century, such as with horses and swords, as well as with men and guns. During the war, new technologies were developed that changed warfare forever, such as tanks, airplanes, and machine guns.

After four terrible years, the war did end. Germany and its allies were defeated. Millions of people had lost their lives, and millions more were uprooted from their homes. People called it "the Great War" and "the war to end all wars."

EUROPE IN 1900

In 1900, the rich countries of Europe controlled world affairs, but they were arguing with each other and were jealous of each other's power. There were seven "great powers": Germany, France, Britain, Russia, Italy, Austro-Hungary, and Turkey. The most powerful of these were Germany, France, Britain, and Russia.

Back in the 1860s, Germany was not a unified country but a group of states. The strongest of these states was Prussia, whose prime minister was Otto von Bismarck (1815–1898). He wanted to create a unified Germany, in which all states were joined, with Prussia at its head. Prussia had a powerful army, and in 1870, Bismarck used it to attack France. Prussia won, and their victory had two important results. First, it united the German states, so that in 1871, they formed a German Empire, led by Prussian Kaiser Wilhelm I (1787–1888). Second, it angered France, which lost valuable territory in the east, Lorraine and Alsace, to Germany. France would remember this loss, and be determined to regain it.

At the end of the nineteenth century, Britain was the most powerful nation in the world. The **Industrial Revolution** had begun in Britain, so the country was ahead of other European nations in growing its wealth through industry. Germany, however, was catching up fast. Its steel industry was growing very rapidly and would soon be the biggest in Europe. The other source of Britain's economic power was trade. The British Empire stretched from one side of the world to the other, and its **colonies** produced **raw materials** and goods that Britain traded around the globe. Another result of all this trade was that London, the capital city of Britain, became the world center for banking and business.

As the British monarch, Queen Victoria (1819–1901) was also head of the British Empire. By the time she died, in 1901, she ruled over one in four of the world's population.

RULING FAMILIES

Just a few leaders held power in Europe. Three of these leaders were closely related, even though their countries fought on different sides in the war. King George V (1865–1936) of Britain, Kaiser Wilhelm II (1859–1941) of Germany, and **Tsar** Nicholas II (1868–1918) of Russia were all cousins. They were the grandsons of Queen Victoria who had ruled Britain from 1837 to 1901. The old queen was nicknamed "The Grandmama of Europe."

These Indian troops joined the war in 1916. They fought for the British, because India was part of the British Empire.

SOLDIERS

More than 2.5 million men from the British Empire fought in World War I. India sent the most at more than 1 million men. Canada sent more than half a million, Australia more than 400,000, and New Zealand over 100,000 men.

A WORLD OF EMPIRES

The British Empire was the largest in the world, but it was certainly not the only empire. At the beginning of the twentieth century, the world was also dominated by the **empires** of Germany, Austria-Hungary, France, and Italy. When international relations broke down and war finally came in 1914, men from all over the world were drawn into the conflict, because their countries were part of these empires.

The British Empire stretched from Canada and the Caribbean in the west, to Africa in the south and India, Hong Kong, Australia, and New Zealand in the east. These colonies brought enormous wealth to Britain in times of peace, through the goods and raw materials they produced. The colonies and the trade routes between them were also defended by a powerful navy of ships. When the war began, Britain's colonies were able to help in other ways. They provided essential supplies of food, raw materials, and weapons to support the war effort. Most of all, however, they sent men to fight.

Austria-Hungary was also known as the Austro-Hungarian Empire. It consisted of Austria, Hungary, Czechoslovakia, Croatia, and Bosnia. It was ruled by a single monarch, Emperor Franz Josef (1830–1916). By 1900, he had reigned for more than 50 years, since 1848. He had named his successor as his nephew, Archduke Franz Ferdinand (1863–1914).

In the southeast of Europe, the Turkish Empire was declining. It had once been extremely powerful, but as it lost control of the countries in the Balkan region, other countries stepped in to take over. This unstable region would play an important part in triggering the start of World War I.

CHAPTER 2

ALLIANCES

Having created a unified German nation in 1871, Bismarck was determined to protect its strong position in Europe. He believed the best way to do this was to make **alliances** with other countries. These were agreements between countries to protect each other if they were threatened by another country. This began a whole series of important alliances between the major countries of Europe over the next 40 years. These alliances played a great role in taking Europe to the brink of war in 1914. With everyone promising to support their allies if attacked, the tension was set to increase. A very serious situation could develop from just a small conflict.

In 1881, Germany, Austria-Hungary, and Italy signed a Triple Alliance. Germany and Austria-Hungary promised to help Italy if it was attacked by France, and Italy promised to help Germany or Austria-Hungary if France declared war against either of them.

Bismarck was not interested in German expansion. He wanted to keep the peace and defend Germany's position. Russia was afraid that Germany would side with Austria, in Russia's conflict with Austria over land in the Balkans. As a result, in 1887, Bismarck made the Reinsurance Treaty with Russia. Both countries promised to remain **neutral** if the other went to war. This was supposed to keep relations calm between the two countries. In 1888, however, the old German **kaiser** died and Wilhem II took over. The new kaiser did not get on well with Bismarck, and dismissed him. He wanted Germany to be a world power.

This is a monument to Tsar Alexander III of Russia (1881–1894). He made alliances to try to avoid war, but also to strengthen his country.

SECRET ALLIANCE

Italy signed the Triple Alliance with Germany and Austria-Hungary in 1881, but it made this treaty meaningless by also signing another, secret treaty with France. In the secret treaty, Italy promised not to help Germany if France attacked.

FRANCE AND RUSSIA

France and Russia came together because they shared a worry about the danger they faced from the country that lay between them: Germany. For a long time, Britain stayed out of the alliance process. They adopted a position that was known as "splendid isolation." In the end, though, Britain realized that Germany's expansion plans were a threat. They had to make alliances with their friends.

France had lost the coal-rich lands of Alsace and Lorraine to Germany in their war in 1871. They were still determined to get these lands back. Russia had been in alliance with Germany when Bismarck was in office, but when their Reinsurance Treaty was not renewed, Russia was worried that Germany under the new kaiser had become a threat. They began negotiating with France. In 1892, Russia and France signed an alliance: if either of them was attacked by one of the Triple Alliance countries (Germany, Austria-Hungary, and Italy), the other would give military help.

The double-headed eagle was the symbol of the Russian Imperial family.

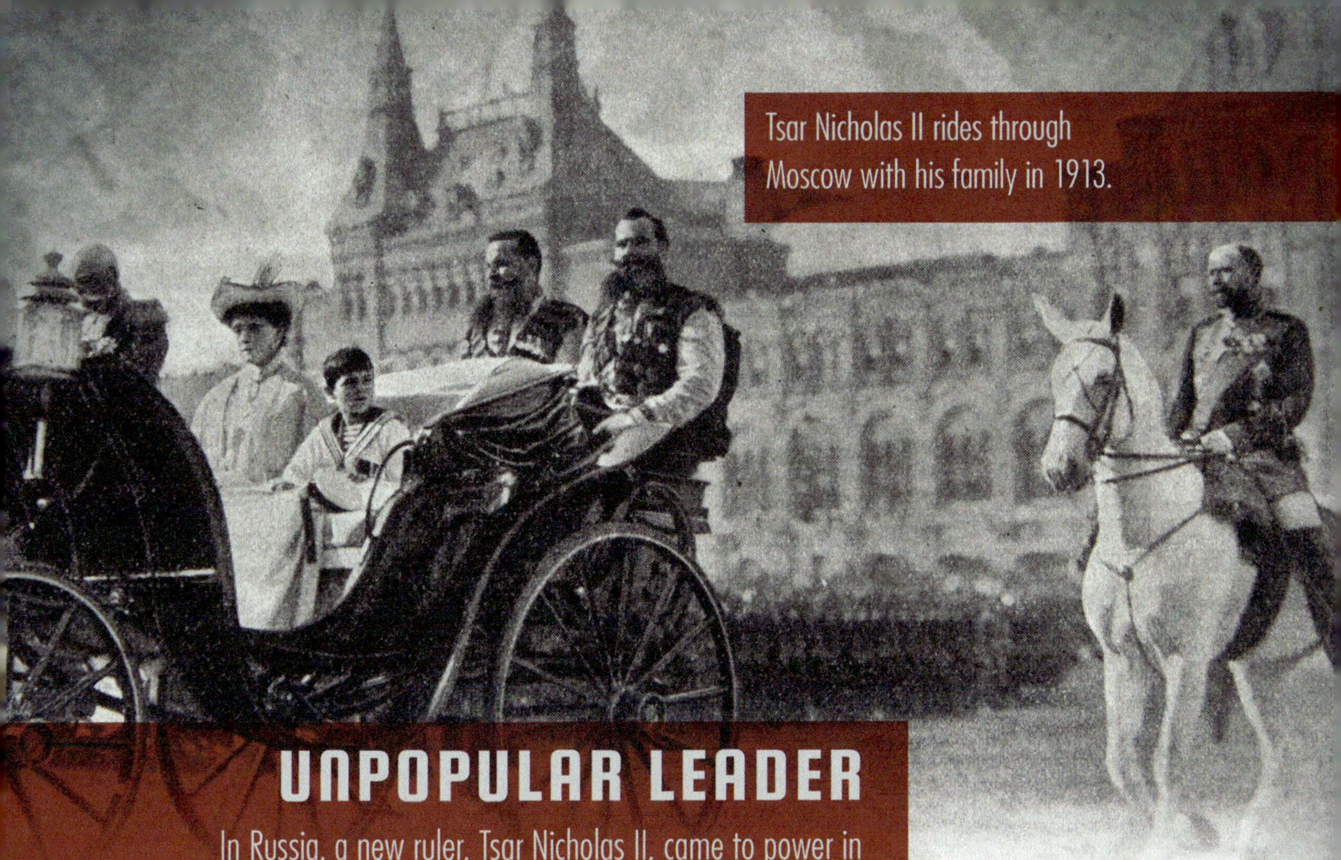

Tsar Nicholas II rides through Moscow with his family in 1913.

UNPOPULAR LEADER

In Russia, a new ruler, Tsar Nicholas II, came to power in 1894, after the death of his father Alexander III. He was an ineffective ruler, who made bad decisions. Although he carried on his father's policy on Russia's alliance with France, the way he governed at home made him very unpopular. He refused to allow the people any say over how they were governed, or to listen to them. When Russia was defeated in a war with Japan in 1904, he became even more unpopular.

The two sides that would go to war in 1914 were now already drawn up: France and Russia on one side, Germany and Austria-Hungary on the other. However, that did not mean that in 1900, war was inevitable. These alliances were intended to keep the peace. They were supposed to make both sides too strong to attack. In addition, the third key player in the conflict, Britain, had not yet joined in the alliances game.

BRITAIN'S ALLIES

Britain's dominant position in the world depended on its empire abroad and on its industrial strength at home. By 1900, it was becoming clear that both of these were threatened by the ambitious plans of Germany. As a result, it turned to Germany's "enemies," France and Russia, for support.

Britain had many valuable colonies in Africa and Asia, which it had acquired during the nineteenth century. Germany's overseas empire was small, but Kaiser Wilhelm II wanted to expand it. In 1902, Britain signed an alliance with Japan, to prevent German advances in the Far East. France did not like Germany's policy either. For example, in 1905 and in 1911, Germany tried to threaten French control of Morocco, in North Africa. At home, Germany's industry was growing very fast. Britain saw this as another threat to its dominant position.

The common threat of Germany brought Britain and France together. In 1904, they signed the **Entente** Cordiale, which roughly translates as the "informal agreement." It did not commit either country to helping the other militarily in a war, but it did strengthen their **diplomatic** relationship. In 1907, Russia joined Britain and France in a Triple Entente. This alliance lasted until the outbreak of the war in 1914.

Germany was now surrounded by three countries that were allied against it. It felt threatened, and was bound to act.

GERMANY'S LEADERS

In Germany, the leaders of the army and navy were very powerful. They had a strong influence over the kaiser. The man in charge of the navy was Alfred von Tirpitz (1849–1930). He convinced the kaiser that Germany must increase the size of its navy, to rival Britain's. In 1900, he started a program of building so many new ships that Britain was sure to be worried, and respond.

This cartoon from a magazine, in 1904, shows Germany (the man at the front) pretending not to care about the alliance between France (the woman) and Britain (the other man), the Entente Cordiale. Cartoons like this are drawings printed in newspapers and magazines to comment on the news of the day.

CHAPTER 3

MILITARY STRENGTH

In 1914, the countries of Europe had been at peace with each other for more than 40 years. However, that did not mean that they had not been preparing for a possible war. In the years before the beginning of World War I, countries on both sides worked hard to increase their military strength.

Britain's navy controlled the seas and was the most powerful in the world. Germany wanted a navy as strong as Britain's, and started building new battleships. Britain did not like this, and in turn decided to increase the size and power of its own navy. In particular, they built a new kind of battleship called the *Dreadnought*. This enormous ship was built in a record time of just 14 months, and completed in 1906. Britain was taking the German threat seriously.

Germany strengthened its navy even further. It built dreadnought battleships of its own. By the time the war began in 1914, Germany had 20 dreadnoughts and Britain had 34. Other countries also responded to this revolution in battleship design. They had to—if they did not keep up they would remain second-class powers. Japan and the United States both started building new, improved battleships.

In the years before the war, Germany also built more **submarines**, which were called U-boats. By the start of the war, it had about 28 U-boats, and more were being built. These were heavily armed, and very effective at sinking enemy warships with their missiles, or torpedos.

A torpedo from a German U-boat narrowly misses a British battleship.

HMS *DREADNOUGHT*

The battleship HMS *Dreadnought* revolutionized naval power in the twentieth century, because it was so much more powerful than any ship that had been built before it. Its armor was 2 inches (5 cm) thicker than other battleships, and it had more guns. These guns could also fire four times farther.

PREPARATIONS

While Britain and Germany were competing for control of the seas, the countries of Europe also began to increase the size of their armies. Although they wanted to avoid war, people realized it may happen, and it was important to be prepared. The trouble was that this "arms race" only made each country feel more threatened by the others. This in turn made war more likely.

In 1908, Russia began building up the size of its army. In 1912, Germany increased its army by 170,000 men. Russia then reacted by starting a "Great Military Program," which increased its army to 500,000 men. In France, every young man already had to spend two years in either the army or the navy. This was called military service. This period was now increased to three years.

Britain had a smaller army than the other big powers of Europe, but it also took steps to improve it. It was reorganized, and made more efficient. Many soldiers were operating in remote parts of the British Empire, such as India. They were

Here, King George V inspects new army recruits. They were soon to fight in France.

Women worked in the factories during the war, like these German women making uniforms.

SUPPLYING AN ARMY

It is a huge operation to create and maintain an army. It is very expensive and very complex. As well as training and weapons, soldiers need food, uniforms, and many other supplies. As the war lasted four long years, every country taking part was strained to breaking point to keep its army going.

defending these lands rather than fighting an active war. Large numbers of them were now brought home to Britain, to be ready for a European war if it came.

By 1914, Germany and its ally Austria-Hungary had a combined army of about 1.2 million men. France's was about 800,000, and Britain's was about 200,000. Despite all this, when the war finally came, it was fought on such a huge scale that no side could have been adequately prepared. After the war, General Douglas Haig (1861–1928), the Commander-in-Chief of the British Army, said:

> *"In the first place, we were unprepared for war, or at any rate for a war of such magnitude. We were deficient in both trained men and military material, and, what was more important, had no machinery ready by which either men or material could be produced in anything approaching the requisite quantities."*

COMPETING FOR CONTROL

In the years before 1914, there were some other conflicts in key parts of the world that helped add to the tension between the major powers of Europe.

Russia had occupied a province in the north of China called Manchuria, and wanted to expand farther. Japan wanted to prevent this happening. In 1904, Japan launched an attack on a Russian military base in China, called Port Arthur.

Japan's defeat of Russia in China surprised the great powers of Europe and made Russia look weak.

SERBIA

In 1883, Serbia had become a kingdom that was independent from Turkish rule. It allied with Russia to protect the rest of the Balkans from the threat of Austria-Hungary seizing control. This meant it was at the heart of the events that led to the outbreak of war in 1914.

They were successful, and to everyone's surprise they carried on winning against the great Russian army. When Japan also defeated the Russian navy in a sea battle in 1905, Russia was humiliated. Japan was now a major player, and Russia was weak. Russia's military weakness made Britain and France more nervous about Germany.

Russia's defeat by Japan also made the tsar look bad at home. He became even more unpopular, and he faced protests from the ordinary Russian people. To improve his popularity, he had to show that Russia could be strong again in a war. This made Russia more likely to join in with a war in Europe.

The other area of unrest was the Balkans in southeast Europe. This region was important because it was of interest to several great powers. The countries of the Balkans included many different nationalities and cultures. The whole region had been part of the Turkish Empire, but by 1900, the Turks had lost control of Bosnia-Herzegovina, Bulgaria, Greece, Montenegro, Romania, and Serbia. They still had Macedonia, Albania, and Thrace.

Russia and Austria-Hungary were rivals for control of the region. Britain was worried about a major power having control over the eastern Mediterranean because it needed free access to the Suez Canal. This was the vitally important sea route to its colony, India.

TROUBLE IN THE BALKANS

The problems in the Balkans grew worse in the years immediately before 1914. Turkey was in danger of losing control over the whole region, and the Balkan nations were anxious to win their independence.

In 1912, four small Balkan nations combined to drive Turkey out of the region: Greece, Serbia, Montenegro, and Bulgaria. Turkey was quickly defeated, and lost all its territories. This was the First Balkan War. Both Russia and Austria-Hungary were now concerned, because the victory made Serbia more powerful than ever. The great powers met in London, and in 1913, a treaty was signed between the Balkan countries that divided up the territory between them. Bulgaria soon decided that it had not been given enough new territory in the treaty, and a Second Balkan War broke out. Bulgaria fought against its former allies, who were joined by Turkish

SLAVS IN AUSTRIA–HUNGARY

One of the reasons why Austria-Hungary was worried by the power of Serbia was that there was a large minority of Slav people in the Austro-Hungarian Empire. About 23 million of their 50 million people were Slavs. They were worried that Serbia would encourage these Slavs to rebel against their rulers. Now that Serbia was even bigger, this danger seemed even more worrying. Serbia's influential prime minister at this time was Nikola Pašić (1845–1926).

forces, too. Bulgaria suffered a crushing defeat and lost even more territory to its neighbors. Some of that territory went to Serbia, which was now much bigger than before.

A powerful Serbia was seen as a threat by Austria-Hungary. Tension remained high in the region. The newly independent Balkan countries felt united as "pan-Slavic" people. They felt that Russia, the greatest Slavic nation, was their natural ally and protector. Russia was keen to encourage them in this, because it increased its prestige. If anything were to go wrong in these countries, therefore, Russia was likely to defend them. Before very long, something did go very wrong.

King Peter of Serbia, who during the war was defeated and forced to retreat in an ox-drawn cart.

CHAPTER 4

THE TRIGGER

After so many years of tension, one day in June 1914 sparked a rolling series of events that led to the outbreak of war.

On June 28, the heir to the throne in Austria-Hungary, Archduke Franz Ferdinand, and his wife Sophie made a state visit to Sarajevo in Bosnia. Bosnia was part of the Austro-Hungarian Empire, but many people there wanted it to become independent. Serbia also wanted Bosnia to be independent. For this reason it was very risky of the Archduke to visit. A gang of Serb nationalist **terrorists** called the Black Hand heard he was coming, and planned to **assassinate** him.

Franz Ferdinand and Sophie were greeted by the mayor of Sarajevo and driven by car toward the Town Hall. On the way, one of the terrorists threw a bomb at their car. The Archduke immediately threw the bomb to one side. Unfortunately it went off under the following car, causing serious injuries, but the royal couple was safe. After their failure to kill the Archduke, the Black Hand gang scattered across the city.

After attending a meeting at the Town Hall, Franz Ferdinand asked to be driven to the hospital to visit the people injured by the bomb. His driver took a wrong turn, and their car entered a side street. By chance, one of the terrorists was standing on the street corner. He was Gavrilo Princip (1894–1918). As the Archduke's car began to reverse, Princip decided to act. He stepped forward and shot Franz Ferdinand and Sophie. The couple was rushed to the hospital, but both died.

The question now was how would Austria-Hungary and Russia react to this assassination? From this tragic event one thing led to another, resulting in a war that would be more terrible than anyone could possibly have imagined.

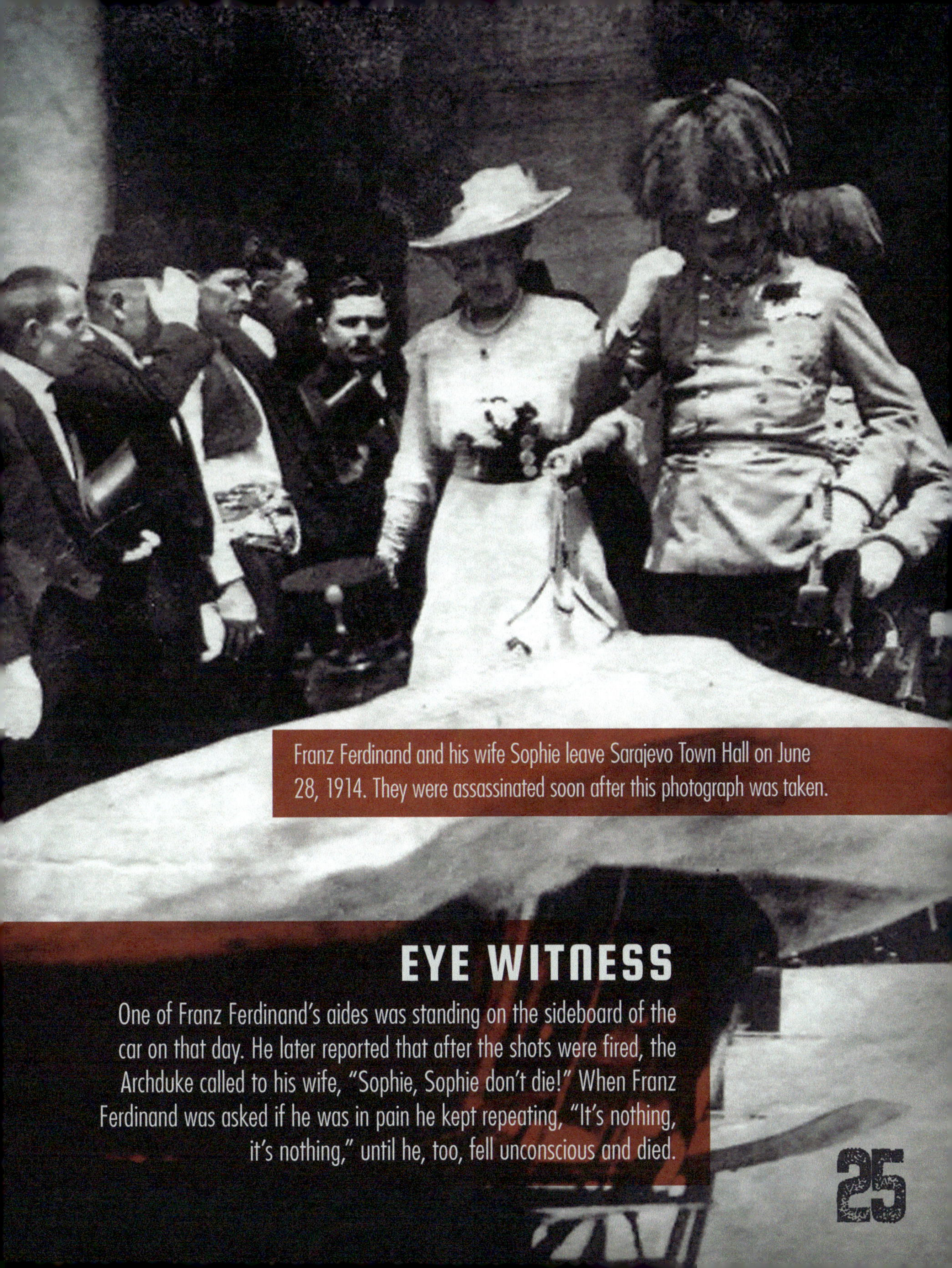

Franz Ferdinand and his wife Sophie leave Sarajevo Town Hall on June 28, 1914. They were assassinated soon after this photograph was taken.

EYE WITNESS

One of Franz Ferdinand's aides was standing on the sideboard of the car on that day. He later reported that after the shots were fired, the Archduke called to his wife, "Sophie, Sophie don't die!" When Franz Ferdinand was asked if he was in pain he kept repeating, "It's nothing, it's nothing," until he, too, fell unconscious and died.

THE JULY CRISIS

The assassination of Franz Ferdinand gave Austria-Hungary an opportunity to invade Serbia and bring it into their empire. They learned that the terrorists had used Serbian weapons. They even learned that the prime minister of Serbia had known about the attack before it happened. In fact, the prime minister had tried to warn the Austrians about it, but his warning was so vague that they did not understand the serious nature of the threat.

Austria-Hungary's military leaders wanted to attack Serbia immediately. The emperor was more cautious. He knew that if he invaded, Russia would join in to support Serbia. He consulted his German ally. The German kaiser gave the emperor a promise of his full military support. This has become known as the "blank check," that gave Austria-Hungary Germany's support in whatever action they chose to take. The kaiser then went off on his summer vacation.

Many Serbians, such as this family, were made refugees when Austria-Hungary eventually declared war on their country.

Kaiser Wilhelm II of Germany was a weak ruler, easily influenced by his military leaders.

GERMANY'S "BLANK CHECK"

Why did Germany give Austria-Hungary the "blank check" of their support? Kaiser Wilhelm II and his military advisers were sure that war would come in Europe at some point, and they wanted it to start sooner rather than later. They thought this would give them the best chance of success, because their preparations were more advanced than their opponents.

The Austrians chose not to invade immediately. Instead, on July 23, they gave the government of Serbia a list of demands. If they would accept them, they would not be invaded. The demands were very harsh, and although Serbia did accept most of them, they could not accept them all. This delay gave Russia time to start mobilizing its army to protect Serbia.

The alliances that had been made in earlier years were now really being put to the test. Russia and France had made an alliance, but would France now support Russia in a war with Austria-Hungary over Serbia? If it did, and Germany joined the war to support Austria-Hungary, would France be willing to go to war with Germany?

These few weeks, in July 1914, were some of the most tense and difficult in all of modern history. The decisions that leaders made would have huge consequences for the future of the world.

WOULD BRITAIN JOIN?

As the political and military leaders of Austria-Hungary, Germany, Russia, and France debated whether or when to go to war, one country remained uncommitted. That country was Britain.

Germany thought that Britain would probably not join in with a war in Europe. This was because Britain did not have a binding military alliance to side with France. If Germany went to war, it would be with Russia and France only. Some historians have suggested that if Britain had said earlier that it would support France and Russia, Germany would have backed away from starting the war. Germany might have told Austria-Hungary to settle its argument with Serbia instead. If Britain had said it would stay neutral, and not support France, Russia and France might have tried harder to find a peaceful solution.

As it was, Britain tried to act as mediator in the July crisis. Russia was preparing its army on the eastern border with Germany. Germany was preparing to strike France first, and win a rapid victory there. It then planned to turn to confront Russia in the east. This plan was called the Schlieffen Plan, after the German who created it, General Count Alfred von Schlieffen (1833–1913). Neither side was interested in Britain's attempts to bring them to negotiate.

SIR EDWARD GREY

The British foreign secretary was Sir Edward Grey (right) (1862–1933). He tried and failed to prevent the outbreak of the war in July 1914. As it became clear that war was about to begin, he famously said, "The lamps are going out all over Europe; we shall not see them lit again in our lifetime."

Sir Edward Grey knew that war with Germany was inevitable and predicted that the conflict would be catastrophic for all involved.

In the end, Britain was forced to act. It was not a military alliance with France that made them join the fight. It was a treaty they had made 75 years before. This was the Treaty of London of 1839. In it, Britain had promised to defend Belgium if it was attacked. Germany dismissed this treaty as a "scrap of paper." They did not think Britain would keep to it. They were wrong.

CHAPTER 5

WAR BEGINS

Events now moved very quickly. On July 28, Austria-Hungary declared war on Serbia. Russia did not declare war on Austria-Hungary immediately, but it had promised to support Serbia, and so it began to mobilize its large army to defend them. Germany saw this mobilization as an act of war. They asked Russia to stop. When Russia refused, Germany declared war on Russia on August 1, 1914. A peaceful settlement of the crisis was now impossible. World War I had begun.

Germany's plan was to defeat France first. The quickest route into France from Germany was through Belgium. On August 3, Germany declared war on France. The very next day, August 4, German troops poured over the border into Belgium. Britain now had no choice but to declare war on Germany.

Belgium tried hard to stop the German advance, but it was impossible. Many desperate Belgians literally dropped what they were doing, abandoned their homes, and headed for the coast. Many thousands fled to Britain, where they were given shelter and set up new lives while the war lasted. Meanwhile, in Belgium, their cities were being destroyed. In Britain, people were appalled at what had happened to Belgium. Many men wanted to **enlist**, or join the army, to fight the enemy that had done this. More than 750,000 young British men enlisted in less than a month.

The United States did not join in the war in 1914. Most people were not in favor of joining in with a conflict far away in Europe. Some said it was the United States' duty to side with British and French **democracy** against Germany's aggression. However, President Woodrow Wilson (1856–1924) was reelected in 1916, after promising the United States would not join in.

NEUTRAL COUNTRIES

Some countries in Europe did not take sides in the war and instead remained neutral. These included Switzerland, Spain, the Netherlands, Denmark, Norway, and Sweden. When the war began, Italy was also neutral. Both sides tried to persuade the neutral countries to ally with them. Italy eventually joined the **Allies** in 1915, because they promised that after they won they would give Italy some territory from the Austro-Hungarian Empire.

The Belgian Army was forced to retreat by the merciless attack of the German Army in 1914.

OVER BY CHRISTMAS

Both sides believed the conflict would be over quickly. There would be a few terrible but decisive battles, and one side would be victorious. Germany's Schlieffen Plan was designed to get them to Paris with great speed. Once they had reached the capital, France would surrender. Unfortunately things did not turn out this way.

As Germany tore its way through Belgium, the French army launched an attack in the east on its border with Germany, in an area called Lorraine. In a terrible battle, they were heavily defeated by German machine guns and artillery. Hundreds of thousands of French troops died. Britain sent the British Expeditionary Force over to France to help. On August 24, the British and French armies met the Germans at Mons in Belgium. The Allies suffered another defeat. They retreated back into France, pursued by the German Army.

In the east, the Russian Army invaded Germany on August 17. Germany sent some of its troops to meet this threat. Between August 26 and 31, at the Battle of Tannenberg, the Germans defeated the Russians. About 50,000 Russian soldiers were killed, and 100,000 more were taken prisoner. Russia was driven out of Germany. Austria-Hungary was having less success in Serbia. They were losing in battles with Russian troops, and Germany had to send some of its troops to help them.

BIG GUNS

One reason why Germany was so successful in the first battles of the war was that it had more weapons than its opponents, and better ones. The Germans had about 12,000 machine guns in 1914, while the British and French had just a few hundred. Germany also used huge siege guns. The most famous one could fire its enormous **shells** up to 9 miles (15 km) into enemy territory.

The Germans used these huge siege guns to pound the enemy across large distances.

CHAPTER 6

WAR SPREADS

Japan had joined the war on the side of the Allies, and started to attack German-held territories in the Far East. In Africa, British and French forces attacked German colonies. This was becoming a global war.

Key events of the early months of the war:

1914

August 1–3: Germany declares war on Russia and France.

August 4: Germany invades Belgium. Britain declares war on Germany.

August 23: The Battle of the Mons is fought in Belgium. The British and French retreat southwest, back from the Belgian border, toward Paris. The German Army plans to go around the back of the French Army, to the west, surround it, and defeat it. However, their troops are exhausted and supplies are low. The German commanders decide that the army should move to the east of Paris, in front of the Allied armies, instead of to the west behind them.

September 6: The French commander launches a surprise attack. French and British forces attack the German Army on the Marne River. The battle lasts for several terrible days. The Allies win. The Germans retreat back toward the northeast.

September 15–November 24: In the "race to the sea," the retreating Germans are pursued by the French and British. When the Germans reach the Aisne River, they stop. They dig trenches into the ground and defend them with machine guns. The Allies cannot break through, so they dig trenches of their own.

These taxicabs and buses are lined up ready to take the French soldiers to face the Germans in battle.

TAXIS OF THE MARNE

During the Battle of the Marne, the French Army desperately needed more troops, and fast. On September 7, thousands of troops were loaded into 600 taxicabs in Paris, and driven to the battlefield.

THE WESTERN FRONT

Between the Aisne River and the coast there was a large area of land that both sides wanted to control. This was Flanders. The German and Allied armies fought a series of terrible battles here, along what came to be known as the Western Front, because it was to the west of Germany.

As each side tried to move forward, they were blocked by the other side. The armies attacked each other with weapons, leading to an enormous loss of life. One of the worst battles was outside the town of Ypres, in October and November 1914. About 250,000 soldiers on all sides were killed in this battle. No one who survived the first Battle of Ypres would ever forget it.

As winter came, the ground froze hard and neither side could move forward. The two sides were stuck in their trenches, along a front line that stretched for hundreds of miles from the coast in the north to the border with Switzerland in the south.

Life in the trenches was very hard. It was often wet, and always cold. It was also very dangerous. The trenches were just deep enough to hold a man of average height, but too often soldiers were killed by enemy gunfire if they just raised their head above the trench wall. The area of ground between the trenches of each side was called "no-man's land." It was churned to mud by exploding shells and by the boots of so many men. If one side launched an attack and sent its men "over the top" of a trench toward the enemy, no-man's land would be littered with the bodies of dead soldiers. It was very dangerous to try to bring these back to the trenches.

The city of Ypres in Belgium was reduced to ruins by the four terrible battles that were fought there during the war. After the war was over, all the old buildings were rebuilt, including the medieval cathedral.

CHRISTMAS TRUCE

On December 25, 1914, the guns fell silent for a short while. German soldiers had been singing carols the night before. Now a few soldiers on both sides climbed out of their trenches without their weapons. They shook hands and exchanged gifts of chocolate, tobacco, and buttons from their uniforms. More soldiers joined in. There were even games of football. All too soon, though, the **truce** was over and the fighting began again.

STALEMATE

By the spring of 1915, Europe was stuck in a stalemate of trench warfare. Neither side could defeat the other. The hundreds of thousands of soldiers on the Western Front would never have imagined that they would be living and fighting in those muddy holes for years.

Through 1915 and 1916, the two sides continued to destroy each other along the Western Front. Although they could see that neither side was gaining much ground, the generals believed that their enemy would back down if they just kept

Life in the trenches was miserably cold, wet, and cramped. It was the same for the armies on both sides.

THE WAR AT SEA

The war was also being fought at sea. The British navy was bigger than the German Navy, but the Germans had U-boats, which were submarines that they used to sink enemy ships. They attacked trading ships as well as warships, to cut off the Allies' supplies. In May 1916, the two navies faced each other in a major battle at Jutland in Denmark. Both sides lost many ships and men, and both claimed victory. This was the last big naval battle of the war.

on bombarding them. In July 1916, at the Battle of the Somme, 750,000 British soldiers attacked the Germans along an 18-mile (30 km) line. About 125,000 of them were killed in fighting that lasted until November.

Meanwhile in the east, Serbia was defeated by Austria-Hungary and Germany. Russia was fighting the Central Powers along a wide stretch called the Eastern Front. Russia had some success at first, but there were serious problems at home. In 1917, the Russian Revolution overthrew the tsar and brought a radical new government to the country. This government did not want the war, and signed a separate peace treaty with Germany.

The Allies were also fighting beyond Europe. British, French, Australian, and New Zealand troops fought the Turks in the Dardanelles. This was a narrow channel of water that connected the Black Sea to the Mediterranean. The Turks had been fighting Russia here. The campaign was a disaster. The Allies lost thousands of men and had to retreat. In 1916, the British were also defeated by the Turks in territories that today are in Iraq.

THE UNITED STATES

For the first two years, the United States stayed out of the war. Gradually, more Americans began to think their country should join. In 1915, a German U-boat sank a British luxury passenger liner, the *Lusitania*, on its way from New York City to Britain. More than 120 U.S. citizens were among the 1,193 who died. This angered many Americans.

By 1917, the Allied campaign was really under pressure. Food supplies were low because German U-boats sunk supply ships. When U-boats sank U.S. ships sending arms to the Allies, American public opinion favored joining the war.

The final push to war came in January 1917. Germany's foreign minister sent a secret message to the American ambassador in Mexico. It ordered him to form an alliance between Germany, Mexico, and Japan against the United States. Germany hoped that if the United States had this problem with a neighbor, they would not join the war in Europe. The British found out about the telegram, and told

The sinking of the *Lusitania* turned people's opinion in the United States more in favor of joining the war.

U.S. troops arrived in France but it was several months before they were ready to join the fighting.

GENERAL PERSHING

The U.S. Army in Europe had its own commander, General John Pershing (1860–1948). He soon saw the urgent need for more forces. Within a few weeks of arriving, he put in a request for an army of 1 million men from home. A week later, he changed that request to 3 million men. In the end, about 2 million Americans went to fight.

the U.S. government about it. When the story appeared in the newspapers, people were outraged. In April 1917, the United States declared war on Germany. President Woodrow Wilson said:

> *"We are but one of the champions of the rights of mankind . . . The world must be made safe for democracy."*

Thousands of U.S. troops sailed to Europe to train and then fight. It took months before they could have an impact on the fighting, but the fact that the United States had joined the war strengthened the Allies' morale. Also, the generals could plan for a new offensive push on the Western Front.

PEACE AT LAST

Could the deadlock now be broken at last? In March 1918, the new Russian government signed a peace treaty with Germany. The terms were very harsh, and Russia lost a lot of territory from its former empire. Some German people began to think their commanders would prefer to fight on, and conquer more land, rather than find a way to peace. Unrest began to grow, and some factory workers went on strike. In the Middle East, the British were successful in their battle with the Turks, who surrendered in September.

BRITISH TANKS

The British secretly developed tanks in 1915. They were originally called landships, but factory workers called them tanks because they looked like water tanks. Because armored tanks could cross muddy and bumpy ground to fire on the enemy, they played an important part in breaking the stalemate of trench warfare. Their design was improved as the war progressed.

These tanks were behind the front line, ready to move up into battle when needed.

As the Allies moved across France liberating the country, they were welcomed by citizens who had suffered years of German occupation.

The German military was happy to move its troops from the Eastern Front to the Western Front. They thought they could win before the American troops were ready to fight. They launched the Spring Offensive, a new wave of attacks. In a series of terrible battles, at Ypres and elsewhere, hundreds of thousands of men were killed on both sides. In July, U.S. troops joined the Allies in the Second Battle of the Marne and forced the Germans into retreat. Then began the Hundred Days, a last Allied offensive that finally brought them victory.

The Allies used a new firing technique to destroy the enemy's guns before battle started. Then the troops advanced, protected by artillery and a new weapon, the tank. By November, the Germans had been pushed right back. The kaiser resigned and fled to the Netherlands. On November 11, German and Allied leaders signed the **armistice**, an agreement to stop fighting. At 11 a.m. the guns finally fell silent. The war was over.

THE WAR TO END ALL WARS?

Why did war break out in 1914? There were long-term causes and short-term causes. The great European powers were competing for dominance in wealth and territory. To protect themselves, they set up a network of alliances. These made some kind of conflict almost inevitable. When the spark was lit in Serbia, the crisis between Austria and Russia was spread by the alliance system into a war that engulfed everyone.

Across northern France and Belgium, large cemeteries of soldiers from both sides killed in the war are still maintained, so their memory can be honored and their sacrifice remembered.

HUMAN COST

Millions of soldiers from around the world were killed during the war. Thousands of them have no known grave. Their names are carved on huge memorials in towns such as Ypres in Belgium. Others are buried in cemeteries across Europe. We still remember them on November 11, each year. Millions more were injured, in both their bodies and their minds. They had witnessed a horror that no one should ever see. The human cost of the war was the worst of all.

In 1918, after so much death and horror, it was difficult for the victors to forgive. When they met at Versailles in France to figure out a peace settlement, they wanted someone to blame. They blamed Germany for turning a small argument into a European war because they had wanted it. This may have been partly true, but it was not the whole story. Most importantly, it led to a peace treaty that was extremely hard on Germany. In the Treaty of Versailles in 1919, Germany was blamed for causing the war and lost a lot of territory, including the lands France had lost to Germany in 1871. They also had to pay huge amounts of money to the Allied countries, to make up for the damage they had suffered. Their army was limited, and they could have no aircraft. Some people at the time criticized the treaty as too harsh. The United States would not agree to it.

The tragedy was that World War I was not "the war to end all wars." The Treaty of Versailles was not an effective way to keep the peace. It made many Germans angry, and it badly weakened their economy. Sadly, it only paved the way for another world war 20 years later.

GLOSSARY

alliances agreements made between states, often to protect each other in a war

Allies Britain, France, Russia, the United States, and their allies ("friends")

armistice an agreement to stop fighting in a war

assassinate to murder a public figure

Central Powers Germany, Austria-Hungary, Turkey, and their allies

colonies countries that are ruled and run by another country

democracy a system in which people can vote in elections to decide who will run their country

diplomatic a way of making agreements in a tactful way with other countries at a high level

empires groups of countries controlled and run by one other country

enlist to sign up to join the military

Entente an agreement or treaty between countries

Industrial Revolution the rapid development of industry using machines and other new technology that took place in the 1900s

kaiser a German king

neutral not joining in on either side in a conflict

raw materials natural substances that are use in industry to make goods

shells metal cases filled with explosives that are fired from a gun

submarines ships that can travel under water

terrorists people who use violence for a political purpose

truce an agreement to stop fighting for a while

Tsar an emperor of Russia

FOR MORE INFORMATION

BOOKS

Fein, Eric: *Weapons, Gear, and Uniforms of World War I* (Equipped for Battle). North Mankato, MN: Capstone Press, 2012.

Kent Rasmussen, R. *World War I for Kids* (For Kids). Chicago, IL: Chicago Review Press, 2014.

Swain, Gwenyth. *World War I* (You Choose: History). North Mankato, MN: Capstone Press, 2012.

WEBSITES

Find lots of information on World War I, including timelines, photographs, and collections of telegrams at:

www.firstworldwar.com

Take a closer look at the locations and details of the major battles in World War I at:

www.pbs.org/greatwar/maps/index.html

Click the links for details on political and military leaders, war heroes, and trench warfare at:

spartacus-educational.com/FWW.htm

For a collection of useful links on the U.S. military experience in World War I visit:

www.worldwar1.com

INDEX